The Heaven Zoo

Story and art by
Deidre J Owen

Digital art created by Deidre J Owen © 2017. Photographic source www.pixabay.com (Creative Commons CC0).
Editing by Michelle Horn at www.excellentedits.com.
Available at www.amazon.com

ISBN-10: 1975677390
ISBN-13: 978-1975677398

This book is dedicated to my favorite little animal lover,
Evangeline Noël.

And a special thanks to my biggest little fans,
Caleb and Kylie.

In Heaven, I plan to ask God for a zoo
filled with all of my favorite creatures.
Spotted ones, smooshy ones, blue, slow, and weird,
so many remarkable features!

I would ask for a
tree sloth
whom I would name
Grungy.

Make sure that you
bring him a flower!

In exchange, he will make his way over to you for a hug!

It might take an hour.

Next,
a giraffe I'd call Paul.

Tall Paul.

Who's the tallest of tall
of ever and all.

His 'cones you may pat!
His back you may ride!

This is Heaven! You won't ever fall.

Pasco Pascal would be

perfectly

poised to

provide you with

penguin

perfection.

Pat-able, pet-able, never regrettable!

(You'll want seats in the "nibbling section.")

I'd have a flamingo named Frances
who dances.
If you watch her, she'll cast you some
welcoming glances.

The animals would gather to see her perform

as she flutters

and tip-toes

and prances.

I'd have a gray goat I'd call Jeff,
Jeff the Goat,
and he won't even smell bad at all!

He'd look on you kindly
as you scratch at his beard,
his weird, gentle eyes full of awe.

A sweet armadillo named Tips would draw crowds when they hear she will sniff your shoelaces.

She'd play in the shower...

...and every half hour
she'd hold silly animal races.

Gaze upon Gaze
and she'd gaze at you back,
her owl eyes keen and intense.

Silently swooping
and diving and looping
she'd wow you with aerial suspense.

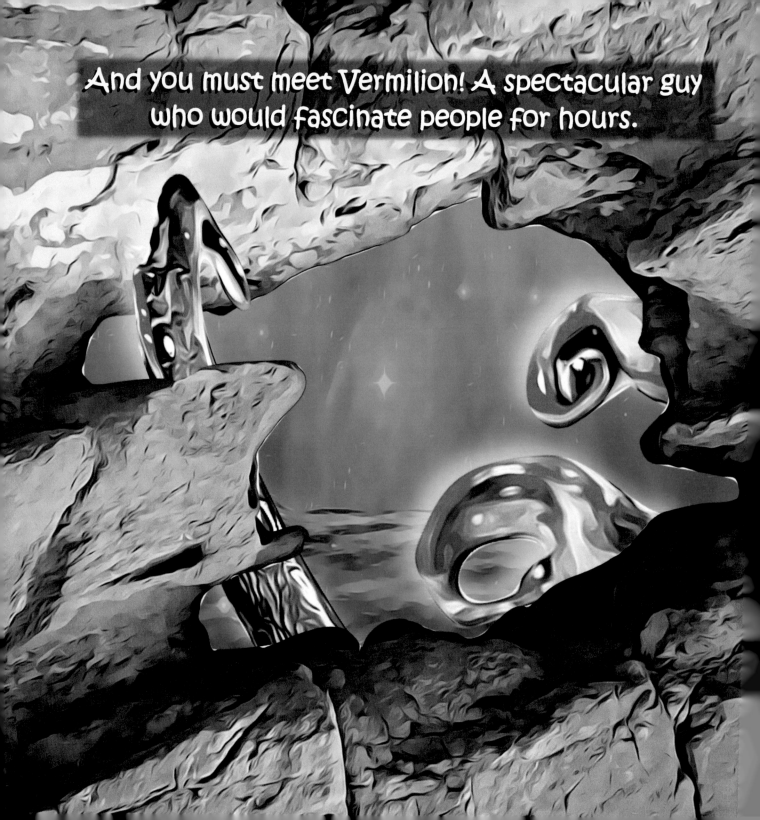

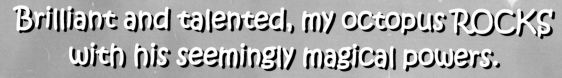

Brilliant and talented, my octopus ROCKS
with his seemingly magical powers.

(In fact, let's just call him my "rocktopus.")

And I couldn't forget the most breathtaking yet,

a peacock of dazzling blue!

His name shall be Fluffy
(by special request)
and his call would be heard
'cross the zoo.

There are so many animals I want to invite,
each one of them special and fun!

I hope you'll come visit.
Bring your favorites, too!

The Heaven Zoo is for everyone.

The end.

What animals would YOU invite?
Draw your own addition to The Heaven Zoo!

Made in the USA
Middletown, DE
09 October 2017